Looking At The Day With Libby

All great
things come
from small
beginnings.

Because I have
an older brother,
I'll always
have a friend.

Sleep?
Who
needs it?

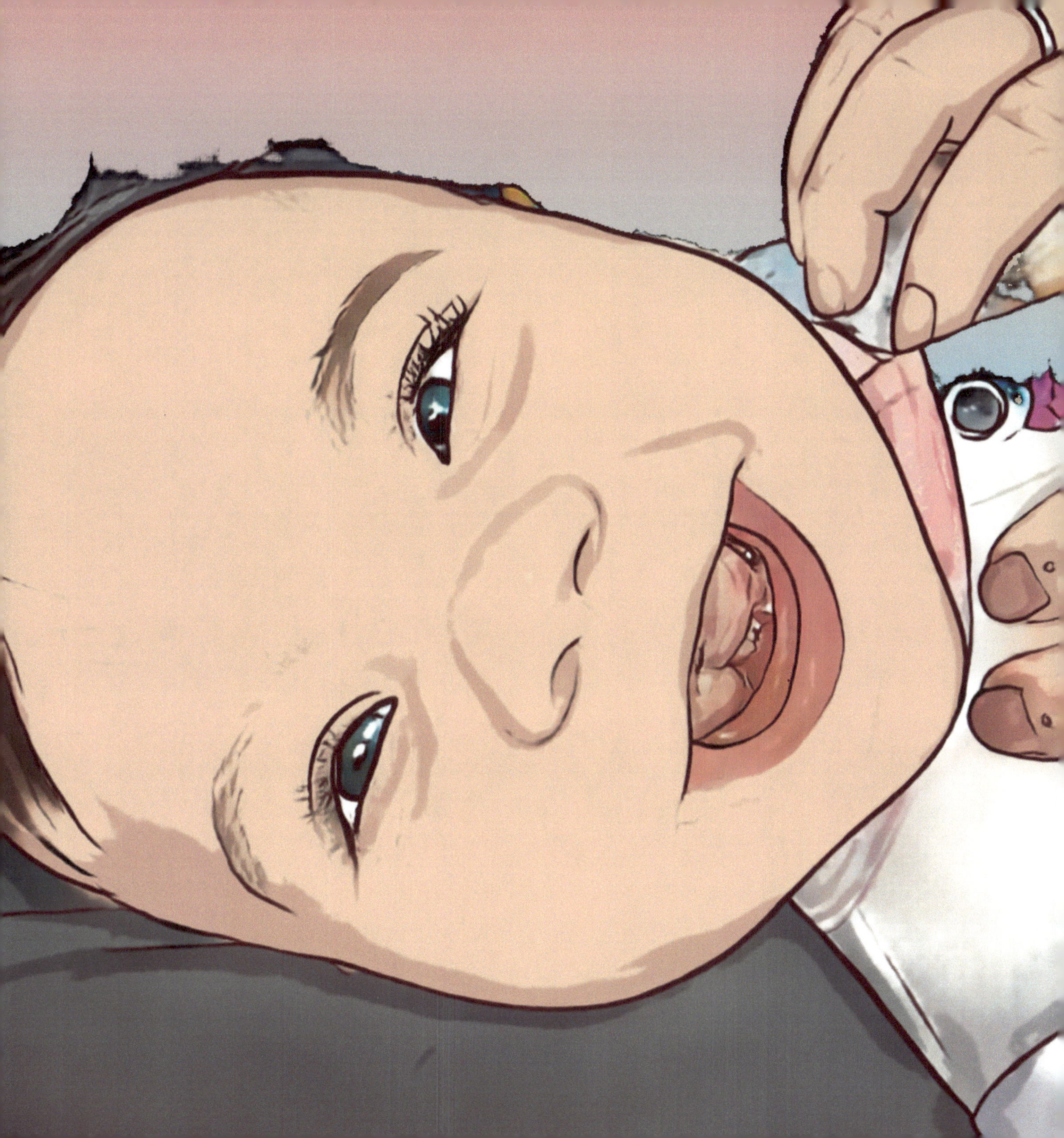

Libby fills the place in your heart that you never knew existed.

A happy baby
like Libby will
spread magic
into the world.

With her adorable smile, Libby will always render sunshine throughout your day.

When Libby
laughs It's
the most
beautiful sound.

Sleep Libby sleep, let dreams come for thee.

An older
brother brings
a bond unlike
any other.

My family is my life and everything else will have to come second.

Libby's heart
touching smile
will make
memories
to forever
remember.

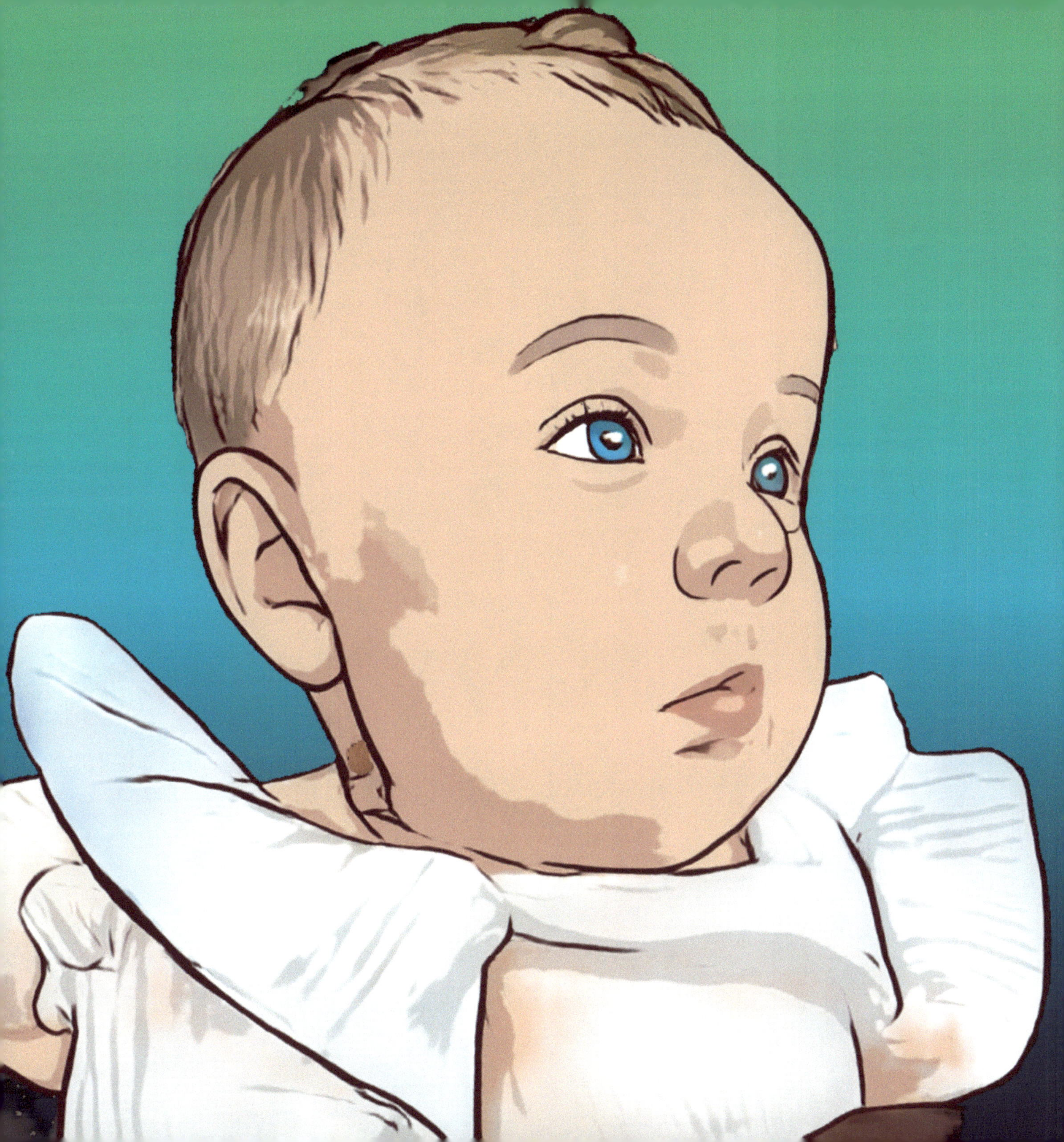

When Libby smiles It's like a ray of sunlight wrapped within your arms.

Though she
may be small,
she is fierce.